Dedicated to Joan's beloved husband, Edwin,
their seven children, ten grandchildren, and
their future generations.

www.mascotbooks.com

The Story of the Curious Elf

©2021 Joan C. Yingling. All Rights Reserved. No part of this publication may
be reproduced, stored in a retrieval system or transmitted in any form by
any means electronic, mechanical, or photocopying, recording or otherwise
without the permission of the author.

For more information, please contact:
Mascot Books
620 Herndon Parkway, Suite 320
Herndon, VA 20170
info@mascotbooks.com

Library of Congress Control Number: 2020909149

CPSIA Code: PRT1120A
ISBN-13: 978-1-64543-197-8

Printed in the United States

The Story of the
Curious Elf

Joan C. Yingling
Illustrated by Ana Sebastian

One Christmas Eve I went to bed.
"Santa's coming!" Mommy said.

As I lay there, eyes half-closed,
Blankets pulled up to my nose,

I thought of all the things I might
Get from Santa, this Christmas night.

As I was drifting off to sleep,
I thought I heard a wee voice weep.

"Oh, how I wish I had been good
And did what Santa said I should.

He's so busy, I wish he knew
That here's an elf with nothing to do.

All the elves are busy tonight
Helping him make his Christmas flight.

O Santa, if I had listened to you
I'd be there now and helping too."

"Each year, you'd always tell the elves 'stay at home! You'll lose yourselves!

For you're so tiny, you're so small
I'd lose you with no trouble at all.'

But last year, I thought it would be fun
To be with you on your Christmas run.

So, after we filled your sleigh that night
I climbed on the back, out of your sight."

"It made me happy when you'd stop
And fill all the stockings to the top.

But oh, that wasn't enough for me
I soon was filled with curiosity.

I wanted to see some girls and boys
And how they liked their Christmas toys.

So once, when you stopped along the way
I hid in a house 'til Christmas day.

The children were delighted and laughed with glee
When they saw their toys and the Christmas tree."

"They giggled and squealed with such delight
I was glad I stayed and enjoyed the sight.

But after a while, I was tired and said,
'I guess I'll go home and go to bed.'"

"When all of a sudden it occurred to me
I didn't know where to go, you see.

I had no map, I had no sleigh
How was I to find my way?

I wandered round the whole year through.
I've been so lonely and...I've missed you."

The whole time he spoke, he sniffled and cried.
'Til I thought he was falling apart inside.

Just then, I heard a noise downstairs.
I knew that Santa must be there.

The little elf must have heard it too
For he ran so fast he lost his shoe.

I followed him though he knew it not.
Even if he did, he wouldn't have stopped.

He was so excited he

leaped

with a bound

And cried:

"Santa Claus!

Look

who

you've

found!"

Santa turned, he looked so surprised

And I'm sure I saw some tears in his eyes.

He picked up the elf and spoke very low,

Put him in his pocket and away they did go.

Now, this might sound fictitious to you
But it really happened, for I have the elf's shoe.

THE
END

TO Melly and Burl –

  May all your days be filled with the
joy and magic of Christmas.

Lydia C—

                    October 14, 2021

ABOUT THE AUTHOR

Joan C. Yingling
(1930 – 2008)

My mother, Joan, began writing at a young age. The earliest writing we know of was a poem about her brother's first step. Throughout her life, she wrote many stories in verse but only a few were saved in a manila folder for the past five decades.

Recently, I pulled that folder out and marveled once again at my mother's talent. Her stories are so creative and imaginative that I felt compelled to share them with readers everywhere.

I was a very young child when my mother first read *The Story of the Curious Elf* to me. Whenever I read the story now, it is her voice I hear in my head. The images her words created in my imagination are much like the illustrations in this book. It gives me great pleasure to share this personal favorite with you. I hope you and your family enjoy it for years to come.

—Lydia Cohn

Lydia Cohn
(Joan's daughter)

IN ADDITION to *The Story of the Can't That Could* and *The Story of the Curious Elf*, Joan C. Yingling wrote many smaller verses for kids. Here are a few of them, and for an extra fun twist, try reading them in funny voices!

Who Am I?

If I go out, I'm still half in
And my house is always where I begin
I can't have friends inside my home
I always feel crowded, though I live alone.
I get tired of moving and I'm awfully slow
But I carry my house on my back, you know
So if you see me, just pass me by
For I'm only a turtle, and I'm awfully shy.

Deedle Duck

Deedle Duck was a funny old duck
And he went for a walk one day
He quacked while he walked
For his quack was his talk
And here is what he'd say.

I'm a funny old duck and I like to quack
I like the rain when it washes my back
I like to rest when the sun shines bright
And I like to sleep when the day turns night.

Bullfrog

I'm a big bullfrog
With great big eyes
I've got a big mouth
And I catch big flies
I sit on a rock
And I croak my song
But I shut my mouth
When a fly comes along.

Recipient of the Mom's Choice Award

The Mom's Choice Awards® (MCA) evaluate products and services created for parents and educators and is globally recognized in 64 countries for establishing the benchmark of excellence in family-friendly media, products, and services. Using a rigorous evaluation process, entries are scored on a number of elements, including production quality, design, educational value, entertainment value, originality, appeal, and cost. Around the world, parents, educators, retailers, and members of the media trust the MCA Honoring Excellence seal when selecting quality products and services for families and children.

First Prize recipient of Story Monsters Ink's Purple Dragonfly Book Award

The Purple Dragonfly Book Awards is a worldwide book competition that was created by Story Monsters Ink to celebrate the best in children's books. Judges are industry experts with specific knowledge about the categories over which they preside. Awards are presented based on originality, innovation, and creativity in both content and design.

Recipient of an Author Academy Award

The Author Academy Awards, presented by Author Academy Elite (AAE), is an award bestowed for literary merit and publishing excellence in the writing and publishing industry. This award recognizes excellence in literary achievements. Entries are reviewed and evaluated on popular vote, social contribution, and overall presentation (cover, content, flow, and originality) by the Academy's voting membership, comprised of best-selling authors, literary agents, and industry leaders.